Barbie™
MYSTERY FILES #2

The Mystery of the Jeweled Mask

D1039387

Want to read more of Barbie's Mystery Files? Don't miss the first book in the series, *The Haunted Mansion Mystery*.

Barbie™

MYSTERY FILES #2

The Mystery of the Jeweled Mask

By Linda Aber

SCHOLASTIC INC.

New York   Toronto   London   Auckland   Sydney
Mexico City   New Delhi   Hong Kong   Buenos Aires

If you purchased this book without a cover, you should be aware that this book is stolen property. It was reported as "unsold and destroyed" to the publisher, and neither the author nor the publisher has received any payment for this "stripped book."

No part of this publication may be reproduced in whole or in part, or stored in a retrieval system, or transmitted in any form or by any means, electronic, mechanical, photocopying, recording, or otherwise, without written permission of the publisher. For information regarding permission, write to Scholastic Inc., Attention: Permissions Department, 555 Broadway, New York, NY 10012.

ISBN 0-439-37205-4

Copyright © 2002 Mattel, Inc.
BARBIE and associated trademarks are owned by and used under license from Mattel, Inc. All Rights Reserved.
Published by Scholastic Inc.
SCHOLASTIC and associated logos are trademarks and/or registered trademarks of Scholastic Inc.

Designed by Peter Koblish
Photography by Paul Jordan, Mary Reveles, Jake Johnson, Mark Adams, Lisa Collins, and Judy Tsuno

12 11 10 9 8   3 4 5 6/0

Printed in the U.S.A.
First Scholastic printing, January 2002

You can help Barbie solve this mystery! Flip to page 66 and use the reporter's notebook to jot down facts, clues, and suspects in the case. Add more notes as you and Barbie uncover clues. If you can figure out who the culprit is, you'll be on your way to becoming a star reporter, just like Barbie!

Barbie™
MYSTERY FILES #2

The Mystery of the Jeweled Mask

Chapter 1

• • • • • • • • • • • • • • • • • • •

DISAPPEARING ACT

"Break a leg, Kira!" Barbie called to her friend as the two girls parted company at the stage door of the Willow Town Theater.

Kira laughed. She knew Barbie was just using theater talk for "good luck."

"Thanks, Barbie," she said. "I'll pass your message along to the cast of the show. Everybody's so nervous on opening night. They'll want all the good wishes they can get!"

"*The Masked Stranger* is sure to be a hit," Barbie assured her.

"I'm keeping my fingers crossed," Kira said. "All the proceeds collected from ticket sales will go to Mrs. Wellington's charity foundation. That's why she's agreed to feature the fabulous jeweled mask in the show. Wait till you see it."

"Mrs. Wellington is very generous," Barbie said. "Not only is she giving the ticket money from tonight's performance to charity, but she's also hosting the jeweled mask masquerade ball at her home on Saturday night. It's sure to be an event to remember. I'm so glad my editor chose me to cover the story for the *Willow Gazette*. This is one reporting assignment I'm going to love!"

"Oh, Barbie," Kira giggled. "You love every assignment! You were born to be a newspaper reporter!"

"And you, Kira," Barbie replied, "were born to be in the theater!"

Barbie remembered the day Kira had been offered a job with the production staff at the Willow Town Theater. "Next stop, Broadway!" Barbie had said.

"I'm happy to stay right here in Willow," Kira had answered. "Let the stars come to us!" And as it turned out, one of the biggest stars of the stage was coming to Willow. Angela Ames was going to headline for two weeks in *The Masked Stranger*.

"I've reserved a seat for you in the third row," Kira said. "You'll be sitting right next to Mrs. Wellington."

"Terrific!" Barbie exclaimed. "I've already talked with her about the masquerade ball. I plan to get there early on Saturday night to see the rest of the mask collection. She has more than one hundred masks from all over the world. In fact, Becky is planning to show some of those masks in an exhibit at the Willow History Museum."

"I know," Kira said. "It's too bad that Becky had to be out of town for the opening night of the show. She was so disappointed."

"Yes, she was," Barbie said. "But she'll be back in time for the masquerade ball. She wouldn't miss an event like that for anything! She's bringing Dan, her old college friend."

"I know." Kira laughed. "And I'm going with Dan's cousin, Jeff. It should be a lot of fun! But the really good thing is that the jeweled mask will be on display there, so Becky will be able to see it up close. The jeweled mask is the real showpiece of the entire collection. It's valued at more than a million dollars!"

"Wow!" Barbie exclaimed. "It certainly will attract a lot of attention."

Kira was reading Barbie's mind. "Don't worry,"

she said to her friend. "We have police officers here, and the cast and stage crew have all been notified that the greatest care must be taken with the jeweled mask."

Barbie smiled and put her concerns aside. The theater was beginning to fill up. "Better get to my seat," she said. "I don't want to miss even one second of the show. See you later."

Heads turned as the tall blond young woman moved across the third row. Barbie smiled to herself when she heard a young man in another row whispering to a friend, "Look! That's Barbie Roberts, the reporter!" Barbie was proud of her job. She'd grown up in Willow and was thrilled to be reporting on news and events in her hometown.

Barbie looked down the row of red velvet seats and saw a lovely woman with snow-white hair seated in the center of the row. Barbie recognized Mrs. Harris Wellington. Beautiful diamond-and-sapphire earrings matched her necklace of perfect teardrop-shaped gems. Her sapphire-blue gown looked as elegant as the woman wearing it.

"Good evening, Mrs. Wellington," Barbie said before sitting down next to the woman.

"What a pleasure to see you again, Barbie." Mrs. Wellington smiled. "I'm so glad you'll be reporting on all the events surrounding the jeweled mask. The more good publicity it gets, the better the turnout will be for the masquerade ball on Saturday. I enjoy reading your articles in the *Gazette*. And you were so helpful to my friend Alfred Willow. He's very grateful to you for solving that mystery for him."

Barbie blushed modestly. "It was my pleasure," she said, thinking back to what the whole town now referred to as the Haunted Mansion Mystery.

"It's so nice to have some of the young people of Willow remaining in the town after their college years are over," Mrs. Wellington continued. "That's what keeps Willow interesting!"

"Thank you," Barbie said. "And isn't it wonderful to have Angela Ames here as well? You must be so pleased that she will be the one to wear the jeweled mask."

Before Mrs. Wellington could reply, the lights in the theater faded to darkness. A spotlight lit the stage, and to Barbie's surprise, Kira came from behind the curtain. She looked worried. "Good evening, ladies and gentlemen," Kira announced. "Welcome to the Willow Town Theater. Due to a family emergency, Ms. Ames has had to leave. She will not be appearing in this evening's performance. We do apologize and understand your disappointment. Appearing in place of Ms. Ames will be her understudy, Diva Denton. Please enjoy tonight's performance of *The Masked Stranger.*"

Barbie's ears perked up as she listened to the audience's murmurs around her: "Who's Diva Denton?" "Never heard of her." "I hope she's good!"

In fact, Barbie herself was surprised to hear that someone named Diva Denton was the understudy for Ms. Ames. She hadn't heard Kira mention that name. And from the moment Diva Denton came onstage, the murmurs in the audience resumed: "She doesn't know her lines!" "Let's take up a collection to get her some acting lessons!" "I want a refund on my ticket money!"

Barbie was embarrassed for the young actress, who moved stiffly around the stage. The only things that held the audience's attention were the glittery costumes and the real star of the show, the jeweled mask. Rubies, emeralds, sapphires, and diamonds on a background of gold damask and black velvet covered Diva Denton's face. Only her eyes and mouth were visible through the field of precious gems.

"It's the most beautiful mask I've ever seen!" Barbie whispered to Mrs. Wellington.

"Thank you for saying so," the woman said softly. "But I'm afraid even the jeweled mask won't cover Ms. Denton's mistakes."

Barbie agreed. In fact, she was already planning her review of the play for the newspaper. The plot of the play was good. It was about a princess under a witch's spell. The princess was forced to go to a strange land, where she had to wear a jeweled mask until a handsome prince kissed her and broke the spell. The lead actor and the supporting cast were well trained and convincing in their roles. The scenery was rich and artistic. Everything about *The Masked Stranger* was wonderful except for the understudy playing the part of the masked stranger!

During the intermission, many friends came over to Mrs. Wellington's seat to tell her how beautiful the mask was. Each one of them had already pledged contributions to the charity, and they were looking forward to wearing costumes to the masquerade ball on Saturday night. Only one of Mrs. Wellington's friends mentioned the unfortunate performance of the understudy, Diva Denton.

"I feel sorry for the young girl," Mrs. Wellington said kindly. "I'm sure she is just having opening-night jitters." Then she turned to Barbie. "Will you excuse me?" she said. "I'd like to get up and walk around a bit before the second act begins."

"Certainly," Barbie replied, smiling. "Your seat will be safe with me."

While the woman was gone, Barbie looked through her program, hoping to read more about Diva Denton. She didn't find the name in the list of credits for actors. In fact, someone named Sasha Davis was supposed to have been the understudy for Angela Ames. The name Diva Denton didn't appear anywhere. Barbie wrote the young woman's name in her notebook and made a note to look up other acting credits the young woman may have had.

The second half of the play was no better than the first half. Diva Denton flubbed her lines, missed

8

her stage marks, and tripped on the hem of her own gown. By the end of the play, the murmurs had changed to laughter. Some members of the audience were even calling the play the best *comedy* they'd ever seen!

As the curtain fell and the audience applauded, the theater suddenly went completely dark. A shriek from backstage shocked everyone. "The mask!" a woman's voice pierced the air from the wings of the stage. "Someone has stolen the jeweled mask!"

Chapter 2

A MYSTERY MAN

"Mrs. Wellington!" Barbie exclaimed as the woman slumped in her seat. The shock of the news that the mask had been stolen had caused Mrs. Wellington to faint. Barbie fanned her and patted her hand lightly.

The lights in the theater came back on, and Barbie's quick first aid revived Mrs. Wellington. "Oh, no," the woman cried as she came to. "My beautiful mask has been stolen. Whatever shall I do?" Her breath came in short gasps and her face was pale. "Mr. Simpson, my insurance agent, advised me against lending the mask to the production," Mrs. Wellington said, holding Barbie's hand tighter. "But I insisted for the sake of charity. I should have listened to him."

"Whoever has committed this crime will not get away with it," Barbie assured her.

10

"Oh, Barbie," the woman said with tears welling up in her eyes. "I'd be so grateful if you could help me as you helped my friend Alfred Willow."

"You can count on me, Mrs. Wellington," Barbie said seriously. "I'll do my best to help bring the thief to justice."

Barbie's words calmed Mrs. Wellington a bit, and she tried to smile. "Thank you, Barbie," she said softly. "Thank you."

Even as Barbie was putting a comforting arm around Mrs. Wellington's shoulder, her eyes were scanning the theater. Two uniformed police officers had rushed backstage and were questioning members of the cast and crew. One of the officers was interviewing Diva Denton. Barbie saw her shaking her head and saying she didn't know anything about the disappearance of the mask.

Another officer interviewed Kira. Barbie saw her friend's worried expression as she pointed toward backstage and told the officer what she knew. The officer took notes and then moved on to question other cast members.

When Kira was finished speaking with the police, she looked out into the audience and noticed

Mrs. Wellington leaning on Barbie. "Oh, Mrs. Wellington," Kira exclaimed, running down the steps at the side of the stage. "Are you all right? I'm so sorry this has happened. We'll get it back. We have to!"

"I hope so, dear," Mrs. Wellington said weakly. "It wasn't going to be the star of this show only. It's supposed to be the star of the masquerade ball as well."

"Yes, yes, I know," said Kira, with tears in her eyes. "I'm sorry, Mrs. Wellington. The police are already investigating leads on the case. We were so careful to keep an eye on the mask at all times. Then the lights went out and the mask disappeared! It all happened so fast. What a terrible evening this opening night has turned out to be. First the star of the play goes missing, now the jeweled mask!"

Kira and Mrs. Wellington tried to console each other. As the two talked, Barbie's attention was drawn to the exit doors. Her keen reporter's eye spotted a man wearing a suit pacing back and forth by the side door. Barbie stood up and watched him carefully. He seemed to be waiting for some-one or something, and he looked very impatient. As Barbie studied the man's nervous actions, a burly stagehand ran up the aisle, and the man in the suit blocked his way.

Barbie eyed the two men as they exchanged a few words. Then, to Barbie's surprise, the man in the suit secretively passed something to the stage-hand. The stagehand pocketed whatever it was and dashed out of the theater through the side door.

"Stop!" Barbie shouted across the aisle. She was certain the police wouldn't want anyone to leave yet. But it was too late. The stagehand was gone.

Meanwhile, the man in the suit glanced over at Barbie and then quickly moved toward the lobby. His attempt to blend in with the crowd made it difficult for Barbie to keep her eye on him. Cran-ing her neck to see above the heads of those in front of her, Barbie raced up the center aisle after him.

"Sir!" Barbie called out when she spotted him by

the drinking fountain. "Wait! I want to speak with you!"

The man looked in Barbie's direction, but his gaze reached beyond her. Barbie swung around to see who he was looking at. When she turned back around, the man was gone!

Chapter 3

• • • • • • • • • • • • • • • • • • •

A CAST OF SUSPICIOUS CHARACTERS

Barbie tried to move forward quickly, but the doorway was jammed with people heading toward the exits. "Excuse me, pardon me, may I get by?" she said as she slid between people in the crowd. Then she saw him. The man in the suit was walking swiftly ahead of the crowd and out the front doors of the theater. Feeling certain he'd be gone by the time she got there, Barbie was surprised to see him standing under a street lamp on the corner, talking with the stagehand!

Barbie backed into a doorway of a closed restaurant next door to the theater. She hid in the shadows and strained her ears to hear what the two men were saying. The man in the suit had his back to her, and he spoke in a low voice. It was difficult to hear him, but the stagehand's voice was louder.

"It's in someone else's hands now," the stage-hand said. "I'll keep you informed. I know where to find you."

"Thanks, Marty," was all Barbie heard the man in the suit say.

Before she could confront the two men, the stagehand hurried around the corner, toward the theater's stage door. The man in the suit pulled out a cell phone. He pushed the buttons and then spoke softly into the phone. Barbie leaned out from the dark doorway and was only able to hear three words: ". . . the jeweled mask . . ."

As the man put away his phone, Barbie boldly stepped out of the shadows. "Excuse me, sir," she said.

The man spun around. "Yes?" he said coldly. His steel-gray eyes didn't blink as he stared at Barbie. There was something unusual about the way he spoke.

Just as Barbie was about to respond, she heard her name. "Barbie!" Kira called from the doorway of the theater.

Barbie turned and looked up the block to find her friend. The man in the suit didn't waste a moment. He hurried across the street, against the red light. Before Barbie could catch him, he got into a black sports car parked by the curb and sped away.

Kira waved at Barbie from the doorway where she and Mrs. Wellington stood together. "Over here!" Kira called.

With a last glance down Main Street, where taillights from the sports car were just rounding a corner, Barbie walked back to Kira and Mrs. Wellington.

"I apologize for disappearing like that," Barbie said. "I was trying to catch up with someone, but I wasn't able to."

Kira looked at her friend curiously. She figured Barbie must be on to something related to the mask, but knew better than to ask questions. If Barbie had something to share, she would let Kira know. "Barbie," she said, "the police want to speak with Mrs. Wellington."

"And I wanted you to be in on those talks," Mrs. Wellington added. "I know you're going to need all the facts to find my mask."

"You're absolutely right," Barbie said, taking out her reporter's notebook.

"Hello, Barbie," a police officer said, striding up to the three women. "I'm sorry to interrupt your conversation, but under the circumstances I have to."

"Officer Cole!" Barbie exclaimed. "It's good to see you." She knew him through her job at the *Willow Gazette*. "Have you met Mrs. Wellington?"

"I'm Officer Cole," the officer introduced himself to Mrs. Wellington. "Good evening, ma'am."

Mrs. Wellington shook her head sadly. "Oh, no, Officer," she cried. "I'm afraid it isn't a good evening at all."

"Well, don't you worry, Mrs. Wellington," the policeman replied. "The thief won't get far with a mask like that. We'll catch whoever it is, but we do need to ask you a few questions, if you don't mind."

"Yes, of course," Mrs. Wellington agreed. "I'd be happy to tell you anything you want to know."

Officer Cole asked for a description of the mask and took careful notes as Mrs. Wellington described it in detail. Barbie did the same.

"On the front of the mask," the woman said carefully, "there are more than five hundred rubies, emeralds, sapphires, and diamonds. All of the hand-sewn stitches are threads of spun gold on a background of gold damask and black velvet. Although the mask is insured for one million dollars, its rare beauty is what I value most. Money cannot replace art, and it has always been my wish to share the art of the jeweled mask with the public."

The officer looked up and smiled kindly at the woman. "Yes, I know, Mrs. Wellington. I guess just about everybody knows about the masquerade ball on Saturday. The mask is going to be on display there, right?"

"I can only hope it is going to be on display," she said sadly. "My entire mask collection will be on display. But the jeweled mask is the main attraction. The charity event was going to be the last opportunity for people to see the mask for quite a while. After the ball, my insurance agent, Mr. Simpson from Burnes and Burnes in London, was going to accompany the mask to London for the Jewels of the World exhibit."

Mrs. Wellington dabbed at her eyes with a lace handkerchief, and Barbie reached a comforting hand out to her, hoping to give her courage to go on.

As the police officer continued his questioning, an announcement came over a loudspeaker system in the theater. "Telephone call for Kira. Telephone for Kira."

"Oh, dear," Kira said to Barbie. "I hope it isn't more bad news. There's been enough of that for one night!"

Barbie smiled sympathetically at her friend. "I'll wait for you here," she said.

Kira excused herself and hurried back inside the theater.

"Well, that about wraps it up for now. We'll be in close touch, Mrs. Wellington," Officer Cole finally said, escorting her to a car where her chauffeur waited.

"Good night, Barbie," the woman said as she slid into the backseat. "And thank you in advance for your help."

By the time the car had pulled away and all the farewells had been said, the Willow Town Theater was empty. All the doors were closed except for one. The police went back to the station, and Barbie waited for Kira. When her friend didn't show up after a few minutes, Barbie went back inside the darkened theater to find her. She walked down the carpeted aisle to the hallway backstage, where the dressing rooms were located. The sound of running footsteps startled her. "Kira?" she said, peering into the darkness. "Is that you?"

Chapter 4

• •

A MYSTERY IN A MYSTERY

The sound of the heavy stage door slamming at the other end of the hall echoed through the whole backstage area. "Kira?" Barbie called, louder this time. "Kira?"

Barbie rushed toward the stage door. She stopped by the dressing room with a star on the door and strained her ears to listen. A muffled cry was coming from inside the room! "Barbie! Help! Barbie, let me out!"

Barbie threw open the door, switched on the light, and scanned the room. Huge bouquets of flowers covered the floor, the table, and even the chair. A banner with the words WILLOW WELCOMES ANGELA AMES stretched from corner to corner on the far wall.

"Let me out!" a clearer cry came from inside the closet.

"Kira!" Barbie gasped. She rushed toward the closet door. "I'm here!" she shouted as she scrambled to unlock it. In seconds the door was open and her friend burst out of the closet. "Kira!" Barbie cried. "What happened to you?"

Tears of relief sprang to Kira's eyes. The two friends hugged each other and Kira tried to speak, gulping breaths between each sentence. "Oh, Barbie," Kira cried. "I'm all right now that you're here. But I was so frightened! Someone locked me in the closet!"

"Who?" Barbie asked, rushing to the door to look down the hallway again. There was no sign of anyone. "Whoever it was is gone now," Barbie assured Kira. "They ran out the stage door just as I was coming down the hall. But how did this happen?"

Kira took a deep breath and tried to speak more calmly. "I came in for the phone call," she explained. "It was Angela Ames calling from New York. She told me that when she arrived there, everybody was fine. There was no family emergency. She said the note she got was a hoax!"

"A hoax!" Barbie exclaimed. "Why would anyone

23

want to spoil her opening night with a mean trick like that?"

"She doesn't know why," Kira continued. "And neither do I. All of my theater connections, from wardrobe people to casting agents to directors, have nothing but good things to say about Angela. Everybody who knows her or has worked with her says she's as good a friend as she is an actress."

"Yes," Barbie agreed. "I know her reputation well. Did she say who she thought might be responsible?"

"No," Kira replied. "She has no idea. That's why she asked me to go to her dressing room and try to find the note. She thought the way the note was worded might give her a clue in solving the mystery."

"Did you find it?" Barbie asked.

"Yes, I did," Kira replied, handing the crumpled note over to Barbie.

Urgent message for Angela Ames: Return to New York immediately. Come to City Hospital room 233.

24

"I was about to leave the dressing room when I heard someone coming down the hall," Kira continued. "I knew it wasn't you. Whoever it was was wearing high heels. I don't know why, but I hid in the closet, thinking it might be the thief coming back for something else."

"Is anything missing?" Barbie asked, looking around the room.

"I don't think so," Kira said, looking around carefully. "Everything seemed to be in order. But someone definitely came in here, turned the lock on the closet door, switched the lights off, and left!"

"Well, at least you're okay. I guess I'd better get you home, though. You must be exhausted!"

"It has been a long, long night," Kira agreed. "First the understudy, Sasha, called in sick. Then Angela Ames was called out of town. Then that terrible actress Diva Denton stepped up and said she knew all the lines and could stand in for Angela. And worst of all, the mask is gone. I don't know what to do about the show now. Certainly Diva Denton can't go on again. I've canceled tomorrow's performance so we can get this sorted out."

"I had a feeling you wouldn't have chosen her to be the understudy," Barbie said. "I didn't see her name listed in the credits. And I'm afraid you're right to cancel tomorrow's performance until things can get back to normal here," Barbie said sympathetically.

Kira smiled as best she could. "But, as we say in show business, the show must go on! And it will . . . eventually."

Barbie dropped off Kira at her house with a promise to call her in the morning. At her own home, Barbie stayed up even later, working on her story for the newspaper. But first she reviewed the notes in her reporter's notebook.

- Stolen: Jeweled mask valued at $1,000,000; more than 500 gems, gold threads, soft velvet and satin on underside.
- Owner: Mrs. Harris Wellington
- Insurance company: Burnes and Burnes in London; agent Mr. Simpson will accompany mask to London.
- Clues to follow up on: Angela Ames's sudden disappearance

- Diva Denton — who is she?
- Marty the stagehand and the man in the suit — what is their connection? What did the man in the suit give to Marty? What did Marty mean by "in someone else's hands now"?

Instead of a review of the show, the article Barbie wrote was a news story about the theft of Mrs. Wellington's mask. Even with all the excitement of the evening, Barbie made her copy deadline in time for the article to appear in the morning paper.

When at last she put her head down on her pillow, all the names and clues from the events of the evening swirled around in her mind. Barbie drifted off to sleep, but her usually pleasant dreams were troubled. Her head was filled with visions of the beautiful jeweled mask floating just out of her reach.

Chapter 5

• • • • • • • • • • • • • • • • •

DIVA DENTON

Barbie awoke with Kira's words in her head: *The show must go on!*

She's right, thought Barbie. It was a new day, and Barbie was determined to do everything possible to help Mrs. Wellington get the mask back — and help Kira get the show back onstage.

Over breakfast, Barbie studied her notes from the night before. The name Diva Denton jumped out at her from the notebook page. She was curious about the understudy's understudy. Wouldn't Diva Denton have good reason to want Angela Ames out of the way for opening night? It would be her chance to become a star!

Barbie checked her watch and saw that it was late enough to call Kira. "Want to do some detective work with me?" Barbie asked, the instant her friend picked up the phone.

"Well, good morning to you, too!" Kira laughed.

"I'm sorry," Barbie apologized. She had to laugh herself. "But I was sure your morning would be even better than good if we got right on the case together. I'll pick you up in fifteen minutes, okay?"

"I'll be ready," Kira said. "But where are we going?"

"I don't really know — unless you can tell me where Diva Denton lives," Barbie said. "Have you got her home address?"

"I'll have it by the time you get here," Kira assured her friend. "See you soon."

When Barbie pulled her red convertible into Kira's driveway, her friend was already halfway out the door. She got into the car and presented Barbie with a slip of paper. "Here's the address you want. I have to be at the theater this afternoon, but I can go there with you this morning."

Barbie read the address: *62 Riverview Road, apartment 2.* "I know right where that is," she said, heading the car toward the town center. She drove past the Willow History Museum, the *Willow Gazette* offices, the Willow Town Theater, and down to the very end of town. Turning left down a bumpy road, she drove about five miles out and came to an apartment complex sorely in need of a paint job.

Barbie pulled up to the crumbling curb and parked. Together, she and Kira walked to the door of Diva Denton's ground-floor apartment. They could hear a television game show at full volume. Barbie knocked and waited. After a few seconds she knocked again, louder this time. The door swung open, and a middle-aged woman with red lipstick and bright orange hair squinted at her surprise visitors. "Yeah?" she said. "What can I do ya for?"

"I'm Kira from the Willow Town Theater, and this is my friend Barbie," Kira said. "We're looking for Diva Denton."

"I knew this day would come sooner or later," the woman said, smiling broadly. Red lipstick speckled her yellowed teeth. "The Willow Town Theater is finally getting some sense into their heads! At last they recognize a real star when they see one! So you're lookin' for Diva Denton, eh? Well, come on in!"

Barbie and Kira were startled by the woman's easy invitation. "Is Diva Denton here?" Barbie asked.

"You're lookin' at her, honey!" the woman said in a booming, friendly voice. She bowed deeply and blew three silent kisses to an imaginary audience. "Haven't been called that for more years than I'd care to say, though."

Kira and Barbie exchanged looks of total surprise. "No," Kira said. "We're looking for the *actress* Diva Denton."

"That's me!" the woman crowed. "Actress, dancer, singer, you name it. I can do it all."

Barbie and Kira smiled. The woman was likable — she was a real character. "Well, Ms. Denton," Barbie said politely, "the Diva Denton we're looking for has dark hair and is about twenty-two years old."

"Oh!" the woman said, disappointment covering her face. "It must be my daughter, Trixie, usin' my name again. Can't say as I blame her. But what's she up to now? It sure can't be acting. Trixie's no actress, I can guarantee that! *I'm* the actress. Used

31

to be on the stage two towns over. 'Course, that was years ago, but I've never lost my flair for doin' a little tap dance and singin' a song if I'm asked."

"Excuse me," Barbie said. "But does your daughter work at the Willow Town Theater?"

"In her dreams, maybe." The woman laughed. "Or maybe I should say in my dreams *for* her. No, my Trixie works in the warehouse district on the other side of town. She's a clerk down at Ziegfield's Costume Company."

"That's the costume company the town theater uses. But she does live here, right?" Kira asked.

"She does, and I'm glad to have her here. She's a good girl, and if she has the good sense to use my stage name, she's an even better girl than I thought!" Diva said. "But hey, would you two gals like a glass of lemonade or something? It's nice to have company to watch TV with."

"I'm afraid we can't stay," Barbie said politely. "We have a lot to do this afternoon."

The woman gave Kira a raised-eyebrow look. "Hey," she said. "Did you say you're from the town theater? Guess you had some excitement down there last night, eh? Saw the headline in the

Gazette this morning. What a story! Poor woman, losing a gorgeous thing like that. Give her my sympathy if you see her, will ya?"

"I certainly will, Ms. Denton," Kira said, backing toward the door.

"Aww, call me Diva," the woman said. "I'll tell Trixie you were looking for her. And don't be a stranger, okay?"

"Okay, Ms. . . . uh . . . Diva," Kira said on the way out. "Thank you for speaking with us."

"Any time," Diva replied, closing the door.

Barbie and Kira heard the volume go back up on the TV as they returned to the car.

"Well, that sure was interesting!" Barbie exclaimed, turning the key in the ignition. "And to think Mrs. Wellington thinks it's the young people in Willow who keep the town interesting! She should meet Diva Denton!"

"Where to now?" Kira asked. "Never mind. Don't tell me. I know you too well. We're going to . . ."

"The warehouse district!" they said together. It was time to have a talk with Ms. Trixie Denton.

Chapter 6

• • • • • • • • • • • • • • • • • • • •

SURPRISE SIGHTINGS

On the drive across town, the two friends discussed what they'd just learned about the understudy's understudy. "I can't believe she had the nerve to fill in at the last minute like that," Kira said. "And I'm sad to say her mother is right about one thing — she isn't an actress!"

Barbie smiled. "Perhaps she was just trying to make her mother's dream come true. I certainly hope there's nothing more to it than that."

The car bumped along the road and crossed over the end of Main Street. "The warehouse district is one part of this town I've never cared for much," Kira said.

"I know what you mean," Barbie agreed. "It always seems more like a ghost town, with no restaurants or stores to speak of. Just big warehouses and loading docks. I feel safer in sections of town where there are more people out and about."

"There are always so many cars parked, but you never see the people who drive them!" Kira said.

Barbie slowed her car and turned down a sooty road called Industrial Drive. The wide street was littered with old newspapers, cans, boxes, and other trash. The large warehouse buildings on either side loomed, casting huge shadows across the road.

"I see it!" Kira cried out, spotting a sign that read ZIEGFIELD'S COSTUME COMPANY.

"Good eyes, Kira," Barbie said, following the sign down a narrow alley.

As Barbie steered the car, Kira read all the signs identifying the tenants of each building. Northeast Box Company Storage, Lotsa Lumber Yard, G & G Supplies, Atlas Equipment Rentals, and, finally, the costume company. "Here it is, Barbie," Kira said. "Who would have thought that such beautiful costumes could come from a place that looks like this?"

"Haven't you been here before?" Barbie asked.

"No," Kira replied. "We order what we need.

Then Marty, one of the stagehands, does all the costume pickup and delivery for us."

Barbie had just unfastened her seat belt when a car suddenly pulled out of a hidden driveway next to the Ziegfield Costume Company and nearly crashed into the front of Barbie's car! Luckily, it was going slowly, cruising through the warehouse district. But as soon as the driver saw Barbie, the car sped out of sight. "Hey!" Barbie cried out. "I know the man driving that car!"

"You do? Who is it?" Kira asked.

"It's the man in the suit. I'm sure of it. He was at the theater last night," Barbie explained. "He was talking to your stagehand Marty! What's he doing down here, I wonder?"

"Besides almost causing an accident, you mean?" Kira asked. She was a little shaken by the near miss.

Barbie sat still for a moment, thinking. "Oh, well," she finally said. "Let's check out the store. In fact, maybe I'll find a costume for the masquerade ball. I haven't had a free minute to even think about that yet."

Kira giggled. "You can always go as a girl detective," she said.

"What does a girl detective wear?" Barbie asked, laughing.

"She wears the same thing a girl reporter wears!" Kira joked.

Before opening the door to the store, Barbie and Kira peeked into the dusty display window. It was filled with feathered hats, velvet capes, old-fashioned gowns, and all kinds of masks, from monstrous to magnificent.

"Let's go inside," Barbie said. She turned the knob on the door and pushed it open. A loud roar of a lion greeted them and also alerted the store-keeper that someone had stepped into the store. The girls jumped at the surprising sound, then giggled at their own fright.

"It's just a sound-effects recording," Kira explained. "This place supplies us with stage props and all kinds of recordings as well as costumes." She closed the door, and the lion roared again.

"I'll be right with you," a girl called from a curtained back room. She was muttering behind the curtain, and Barbie and Kira could hear her throwing things around and talking to herself or to someone. "Look at this mess!" *SLAM!* "It's a wreck back here." *BANG!* "Whatever happened to Mr. Ziegfield's 'neat and tidy' rules?" *CRASH!*

As Barbie and Kira waited for the storekeeper to come out, they studied their surroundings. Three walls and the ceiling were decorated with theater posters, masks, stage props, and costumes. Most interesting to Kira, though, was the wall behind the counter. It was covered with glittery and sequined masks of all shapes and sizes.

As they marveled at all the different props and costume accessories, they were again startled by the roaring lion as the door behind them opened. Before they saw who had come in, Trixie Denton came out from behind the curtain. "What are *you* doing here?" she exclaimed angrily, looking past Barbie and Kira.

Barbie and Kira turned around and found themselves face-to-face with Marty the stagehand!

Chapter 7

• • • • • • • • • • • • • • • • • • •

ZIEGFIELD'S COSTUME COMPANY

"I was hoping I'd never see you again," the girl shouted at Marty. "You ruined all my chances of working in the theater! I should never have listened to you!"

"Whoa, whoa, whoa!" Marty protested. "You were great! You played the role just like I knew you would."

Trixie calmed down. "Really?" she said. "Do you really think so?"

"Sure I do! You just need a little more practice, that's all," he assured her.

Marty was stepping toward Trixie, when he noticed Kira. "Oh, hey, Kira!" he said, suddenly nervous. "How are you doing? I heard we're not doing a show tonight, but we'll be back in business soon.

Bad night last night, but things will get better, you'll see."

The man was quite cheerful, perhaps a little too cheerful, considering all the things that had occurred the night before. Barbie wanted to ask him about his encounter with the man in the suit just after the mask disappeared. And was it just a coincidence that they were both down in this warehouse district at the same time? The black sports car had left just minutes before! But Barbie didn't have a chance to question him. He was already explaining why he was at the store.

"I came down here," he said, "hoping I could find another mask to stand in for the real one. The show must go on, right? They've got plenty of masks to choose from here. But look, you two were here first, so go ahead. I'll come back later."

"No, no," Barbie started to say. "I wanted to ask you —"

"That's okay," Marty said. "I insist." He backed toward the door and disappeared through it.

Barbie was suspicious. Marty seemed in an awful hurry to leave. She thought of following him,

40

but before she could act, the girl behind the counter turned her attention to Kira and Barbie. "Hello," she said.

"Hello, Trixie," Kira replied.

"Oh, so you know my real name?" The girl looked disappointed. "But Diva Denton sounds so much better, don't you think? It's a real stage name that I got from a former actress."

"Your mother," Barbie added.

The girl blushed. "You met my mother? Yes, that's her — Diva Denton, entertainer *extraordinaire*. She can be embarrassing sometimes, but she's a great actress."

Barbie smiled. There was something likable about the girl, just like her mother. Barbie hoped she was as innocent as she seemed.

"I know you're coming to tell me not to ever come back to your theater, right?" Trixie said to Kira. "I didn't mean to mess up things. I tried my best. I'm just not an actress."

"But what gave you the idea that you could fill in for Angela Ames?" Kira asked.

"Marty made me think I could do it," Trixie said.

"I met him one day when he came in to get costumes for *The Masked Stranger*. I helped carry things out to his van. After that, he invited me to come around to the theater and watch rehearsals whenever I wanted to. I came every day and that's how I learned the lines for the show." She blushed. "Well, I almost learned them, I mean. I'm not good at remembering things. That's why my mother always says I should stick to renting out costumes and forget about wearing them. "

"Trixie," Barbie interrupted the girl. "Do you remember what you did with the mask after the last scene?"

"I didn't even know it was valuable," Trixie said. "I thought the mask was the one they used in all the rehearsals. It looked just like it. When I found out it was the real one that was missing, I went back to the dressing room to make sure I didn't mix them up and leave the real one in the dressing room."

"What?" Kira said. "You went back to the dressing room? Did you lock the closet door before you left?"

"Yes, I went back," Trixie explained. "And I locked the closet door out of habit. You know, working here, I'm usually the last one to leave. It's my job to make sure every door is locked."

"If the mask you wore in the show wasn't the one used in the rehearsals," Barbie asked, "then where is that one?"

"I don't know," Trixie said. "When I went back to the dressing room, I couldn't find it. But we have others like it if you'd like to see."

Trixie disappeared into the back room and came out carrying an open box. It was filled with masks of all kinds. But the one that stood out was a perfect copy of Mrs. Wellington's jeweled mask.

"See?" Trixie said as Barbie picked up the mask and examined it closely. "It looks just like the real one. I just thought the mask I was wearing was this costume mask."

Barbie believed the girl. "I can see how you might mistake one for the other," she said, holding it up over her own face. She stood in front of a dusty mirror hanging on the wall and stared at her masked face. An idea was coming to her.

43

Kira watched her friend. She knew Barbie was up to something. "Barbie," Kira said, interrupting her friend's concentration. "Just what are you thinking?"

Barbie smiled. "What I'm thinking is maybe girl detectives don't always dress like girl reporters. Wrap this one up for me, please, Trixie. I'm going to a masquerade ball!"

Chapter 8

●●●●●●●●●●●●●●●●●●●●●

NEWS FLASH!

Kira didn't dare ask what Barbie was planning. She knew her friend would tell her everything when she was ready to talk. The ride back to town was quiet as Barbie let her idea take form in her mind.

At a traffic light on Main Street, Barbie sat staring straight ahead, waiting for the light to change. She was deep in thought, and it wasn't until a car behind her honked that she realized the light had turned green. "Oh!" Barbie said, startled out of her trance. She looked in the rearview mirror as she stepped on the gas and moved forward. "Kira!" she said suddenly. "It's him again! Don't turn around."

"Who?" Kira said. She did as Barbie told her and stared straight ahead.

Barbie didn't answer. She drove to the next block,

keeping her eye on the black sports car behind her. The man was talking as he drove, but there was no one in the car with him. *He must be on a speaker phone,* thought Barbie. She pulled her car into an open parking space on the next corner and let the man go by.

"What are we doing? Who is it?" Kira asked. Then she saw the black car go around them. "Oh! Him!"

Barbie let the black car get a little bit ahead and then followed it. The man was driving slowly and seemed to be looking for a particular address. Apparently, he found what he was looking for, and he parked his car in front of Eastman's Jewelry Store. Fortunately, another red light stopped Barbie and she was able to watch the man get out of the car and go inside the store. He was carrying a package.

"Kira," Barbie said, turning onto a side street and up to a curb. "Wait here for me, please. I just want to check out something and I'll be right back."

Before Kira could respond, Barbie had jumped out of the car and was hurrying to the corner. Kira watched as her friend disappeared after him.

Barbie kept her eyes on the jewelry store and the black car parked in front of it.

"Good," she whispered to herself. "He's still there." Slowing her pace to a brisk walk, she pretended to be window-shopping as she headed for the jewelry store. When she came to the display window, she stopped and acted as if she were studying the watches, rings, necklaces, and bracelets arranged on a background of white satin. Actually, Barbie was looking past the display case to the counter at the back of the store. A salesman she didn't recognize was waiting on the man with the package. To Barbie's complete surprise, the man placed the package on the counter, opened it, and took out the jeweled mask!

Barbie couldn't believe her eyes. Was the man trying to sell the mask right here on Main Street? She watched as the salesman examined the mask carefully. After a few minutes, the salesman looked up and shook his head. He was saying "no" to something. But the man in the suit didn't seem to want to take no for an answer. He was holding the mask up to the salesman's face and saying something that Barbie couldn't hear.

The conversation was interrupted by a phone call for the salesman. At first, the man in the suit seemed to want to wait. But his patience was quickly worn out. He put the mask back into the box and turned to leave.

Barbie had to decide: Should she confront the man and demand the return of the mask? Or should she follow him to find out where he planned to take it? Following him seemed safer at the moment. He was too big to confront alone.

Barbie ran to her car, but when she got there, Kira was gone. There was no time to spare. The man would get away if she didn't move fast. She'd have to explain it all to Kira later. As she got back into the car and turned the key, she noticed a small crowd gathered on the other side of the street. The people were leaning over someone on the ground. Was it Kira?

Barbie scrambled out of the car again and raced to the other side of the street. To her instant relief, she saw Kira kneeling next to a young boy who had fallen off his bike. She was wiping blood from the boy's knee and trying to comfort him.

The boy's mother arrived on the scene at the same time as Barbie. "Jimmy!" the woman cried.

"Are you all right?" The woman thanked Kira and took over caring for the boy.

"Kira," Barbie said softly to her friend. "We have to go right now."

Kira heard the urgency in Barbie's voice. She quickly said good-bye to the boy and his mother, and the two friends dashed back to the car. "What's up?" Kira asked breathlessly.

Barbie explained what she'd seen and made a U-turn back toward Main Street. She was sure the black sports car would be gone, and she was right. Kira apologized for making Barbie lose the man, but Barbie understood completely. "I would have done exactly the same thing if I'd seen the boy fall," she said. "It's not your fault."

"Shall we go to the police and tell them about the man?" Kira asked.

"Not yet," Barbie said. "I have another plan in mind that I think might work. "I'll see you later, Kira," Barbie said, dropping off her friend at the Willow Town Theater. "Thanks for coming with me."

"You know I wouldn't have missed it," Kira replied, waving as she disappeared inside the theater.

Barbie headed right for her office at the *Willow Gazette*. Now the idea she'd had at the costume store seemed more important than ever. She knew exactly what she was going to do, but she also knew she had to act fast. She parked the car and swept through the newsroom to her own desk. Coworkers greeted her as she breezed by.

"Hey, Barbie!"

"Hi there, star reporter!"

"What's happening, Barbie?"

Barbie answered all the friendly words with a wave and a smile. She had no time to stop and chat with anyone. She had an article to write for the next edition of the *Willow Gazette*. She cleared the idea with her editor, then called Mrs. Wellington.

"Hello?" Mrs. Wellington said into the phone, picking up Barbie's call.

"Mrs. Wellington, this is Barbie. I can't talk long now, but I just need to ask your permission to carry out an idea I have."

Barbie spent the next few minutes sharing her thoughts with Mrs. Wellington. At the end of the conversation, Mrs. Wellington said, "It's a wonderful idea, Barbie. I only hope it works. I'll look for the story in the morning paper."

Barbie sat down at her computer and began to write.

- Headline: Jeweled Mask Found — Stolen Mask Turns Out to Be Fake!
- Willow, Friday: There is good news today for Mrs. Harris Wellington and the Wellington Charity Foundation. The antique jeweled mask believed stolen last night is safe!
- The stolen mask was actually a copy of the original, with a value of only $19.95. To celebrate the good news, the genuine jeweled mask will be worn by a surprise special guest at Mrs. Wellington's jeweled mask masquerade ball on Saturday night. This will be the final appearance of the jeweled mask before it leaves for London to join the Jewels of the World exhibit.

Barbie read over the copy and delivered it by hand to the young man at the copydesk. "Brian, I need this in the late edition," she said. "And if you can get it on the front page I'll treat you to lunch for a week!"

The handsome young man smiled up at Barbie. "No lunch treats necessary," he said, winking at her. "Allowing me to escort you to the masquerade ball is treat enough. You haven't changed your mind about going with me, have you?"

"Not a chance." Barbie laughed. "A date is a date. And besides, you're going to be a big help. I hope you won't mind doing a little detective work instead of dancing."

Brian looked down at his feet and laughed. "Are you kidding?" he asked. "I've got two left feet, so you'll be a lot safer if we don't dance! But detective work? What do you mean?"

"That's for me to know and you to find out," Barbie teased. "See you Saturday. And don't forget, front page for this article, okay?"

"For you, Barbie," Brian replied, "anything!"

Chapter 9

• • • • • • • • • • • • • • • • • • • •

THE JEWELED MASK
MASQUERADE BALL

The circular drive in front of Mrs. Wellington's white-columned mansion was filled with limousines letting out passengers at the big front entrance. A photographer waited for each couple or group to pose for a souvenir photo in their costumes. Each costume was different, and everyone wore a mask of one kind or another. No one could be sure of anyone's true identity.

"Isn't this exciting?" a masked princess breathed into the ear of the masked queen standing next to her.

"Oh, Kira! Is that you behind the princess mask?" asked Mrs. Wellington, who was queen for the evening. "I'd never have known you. Your costume is wonderful!"

"It's a fabulous turnout for your party," Kira said. "It's great to see so many people helping the charity foundation."

"Yes, I'm happy about that," Mrs. Wellington said wistfully. "I only wish things had gotten off to a better start. The jeweled mask was going to be the main attraction tonight."

"Perhaps it still will be," said a voice behind her.

Mrs. Wellington turned to see who spoke and gasped at the sight of the beautiful jeweled mask. "The mask!" she exclaimed.

Barbie lifted up the velvet covering just enough to reveal her identity. "I'm sorry to have startled you like that," Barbie said. "I needed to test my disguise on the person who would know the mask best — you."

"It is a near-perfect copy," Mrs. Wellington agreed. "Even I was fooled for a moment."

"Mrs. Wellington," Barbie said. "I'd like you to meet my friend Brian Chandler. We work together at the *Gazette*. He's going to help me tonight."

"Pleased to meet you," Brian said, tipping his top hat and bowing.

"Oh, I do hope Barbie's plan works," Mrs. Wellington said softly to Brian. "I can't imagine anyone having the nerve to steal the mask while she's wearing it."

"They will if they believe I'm wearing the real mask," Barbie assured her. "Now, Kira, you know your assignment, right?"

"Right," Kira answered. "Becky and Dan are already stationed by the side door. I'm going to join my date, Jeff, at the doors leading to the terrace. Don't worry, you can count on us."

Barbie looked across the room and saw Becky and Dan. Becky glanced over, but gave no clear sign that she recognized Barbie in the mask. Instead, she put a hand up to her white feathered mask and held it there for a few seconds. It was the contact signal she and Barbie had worked out ahead of time.

"And Brian," Barbie whispered, "you know when to turn the lights out, right?"

"Of course I do!" he laughed. "Don't worry about a thing."

"I won't," Barbie said. "I'll be watching from the

landing upstairs. Mrs. Wellington, please go about your hostessing duties as you normally would. I'll wait for you to announce the special guest and then I'll appear and mingle with the other guests."

"I will, Barbie," Mrs. Wellington replied.

"Barbie? One last thing before you go on," Kira said, smiling.

"What's that?" Barbie asked.

"Break a leg!" Kira said, giving her friend's hand a squeeze.

Barbie moved through a back hallway and up a stairway that wasn't visible from the front of the house. She took her place on the landing, where she could see everything below without being seen herself. It was an amazing sight to see. A string quartet played. People danced or talked or ate or simply played guessing games as to who was who. It seemed as if the whole town of Willow was out for the occasion.

Some costumes were better than others. There were soldiers, tango dancers, kings, firefighters, ballerinas, and characters from classic literature, like *Alice in Wonderland*'s White Rabbit and King Arthur's knights in shining armor. The only ones not wearing masks were the catering staff and kitchen workers. Mrs. Wellington had enlisted the help of many to make the ball enjoyable for all.

As Barbie looked over the crowd of masked guests, she saw some familiar faces. To her surprise, Trixie Denton was there in a waitress uniform, serving hot appetizers along with her mother, Diva Denton. And pacing nervously back and forth in front of the buffet table was the stagehand Marty, dressed in a waiter's uniform that was too tight around the waist. His eyes darted from left to right as he watched the crowd carefully, forgetting his food-serving duties.

One guest stood out from the others. It was a man dressed in the uniform of a British palace guard. He wore a simple black mask over his eyes. He was the tallest guest there, but perhaps that was only because of his tall black helmet. He stood alone in a corner, refusing drinks or appetizers offered by the waiters. He seemed to be watching or waiting for something, and it wasn't something on a tray. Even in costume, he was recognizable to Barbie. This was the man she was looking for. The palace guard was the man in the suit!

When the ballroom was filled to the limit, Mrs. Wellington rang a bell to get everyone's attention. She was standing above the crowd on the landing to the stairs. Barbie took her eyes off the palace guard for a moment and turned her attention to Mrs. Wellington.

Little by little, the room quieted down and Mrs. Wellington began her announcement. "Ladies and gentlemen, kings and queens, welcome to the masquerade ball. As you have all read in the *Willow Gazette*, there is wonderful news tonight: The jeweled mask that was believed stolen at the opening of *The Masked Stranger* was, in fact, a fake! The real mask is here tonight for all of you to see and enjoy. It is being worn by a surprise guest, who shall remain nameless until later in the evening. May I now introduce you to tonight's masked stranger in the genuine jeweled mask!"

Barbie floated gracefully down the winding staircase to the delicate strains of violin music. Like a model in a fashion show, she paused at each step and turned her head to show the beautiful mask to guests on all sides of the room.

People were breathless in their excitement about

the beauty of the mask. While they watched Barbie, she observed them. She hoped the real thief had been fooled by her article and would try to steal what they believed was the real jeweled mask.

Barbie's eyes scanned the crowd, looking for anyone suspicious. There was a masked vampire in one corner who stared hungrily at the mask. Was he the thief?

Across the room, a couple wearing black cat costumes seemed ready to pounce on Barbie, scratch off the mask, and run with it to some secret place. Were they the thieves?

Kings looked ready to conquer the mask. Soldiers seemed ready to fight to save it. Was it Barbie's imagination, or did everyone have the same thought in mind — stealing the mask again?

When Barbie's foot touched the last step, the crowd applauded and cheered. Guests rushed forward to get a closer look.

As planned, right at that moment, the lights went out! Barbie felt hands reaching out of the darkness and grasping the mask from both sides. Grabbing hold of the guilty hands, Barbie shouted, "Lights on!" at the top of her voice.

59

Immediately, the room was flooded in light and Barbie was caught with the mask halfway over her head. In one hand, she held the arm of the man dressed as a palace guard, and in the other, she held the struggling hand of a waiter whose uniform stretched tightly across his stomach.

"Marty!" Trixie cried. "What are you doing? Are you trying to steal the mask?"

"Mr. Simpson!" Mrs. Wellington gasped. "What are *you* doing? Are *you* trying to steal the mask?"

"What?" Barbie said. "You know this man?"

"Why, yes, of course," Mrs. Wellington replied. "He's my insurance agent from Burnes and Burnes Ltd. in London. His company insured the jeweled mask! I didn't recognize you in your costume, Mr. Simpson," she said.

"Well," the man said, "I must say it's a bit out of the ordinary for an insurance agent to wear the uniform of the palace guard. But I am happy to be of service to you, madam, the queen!"

The palace guard pulled his arm from Barbie's grasp and grabbed Marty's other arm. He surprised everyone when he reached into Marty's shirt and pulled out the real jeweled mask. "Here's your thief!" the palace guard declared, holding the mask in one hand and Marty's collar in the other.

"But . . . but . . . but . . ." Marty sputtered.

"No buts about it," Mr. Simpson said. "You stole the mask and the proof is right here. This is the real mask."

Barbie was trying to put all the pieces of the puzzle together. "But what did Marty mean when he told you yesterday it was in someone else's hands?" she asked. "I thought he meant that he'd passed the mask on to an accomplice."

Mr. Simpson smiled. "No, no," he said. "I knew Marty had something to do with the costumes. I was asking him to let me know if he found the mask backstage. Now I realize he was trying to throw me off by telling me the mask was in some-one else's hands — he was trying to make me think someone else had stolen it."

Barbie turned to Marty. "So it was you who sent the note to Angela Ames, then?"

Marty held his mouth tightly closed. He seemed unwilling to reveal anything.

Then Trixie spoke up. "Now I know what he was up to," she said. "He gave me the note to deliver to Ms. Ames. He told me it was important and made me think I was doing something that really mattered. I didn't know it was a fake note." Trixie had tears in her eyes. She looked very upset.

"I know you didn't realize you were helping the thief," Barbie said.

"Of course she didn't!" Diva Denton spoke up for her daughter. "She may not be an actress, but she sure isn't a thief!" She turned on Marty then and spoke right into his face. "Now listen, mister," she said. "You should have never brought my daughter into this mess. She was innocent and she still is and you'd better make sure you say it now, loud and clear!"

Marty was obviously shaken up by the scolding from the real Diva Denton. "Nah," he said, giving up completely. "Trixie didn't know anything. I'm the one who wrote the note to Ms. Ames. I knew that Ms. Ames could tell the difference between the two masks — the real one is much heavier. I wanted her out of the way. I'm the one who took the mask. I thought I could sell the gems and be set for the rest of my life."

A man in a knight costume stepped forward and handcuffed Marty. It was Officer Cole! "Good work, Barbie," he said, turning to the girl who had used her reporter skills to trap the thief. "Looks like you've done it again!"

"Hear, hear! A job well done," the palace guard said to Barbie. "You certainly fooled the thief."

"And *you* certainly fooled me!" Barbie laughed. "I've been watching you since the night of the play!"

"Yes, I know," said Mr. Simpson. "And I believe we were both watching Marty."

Barbie had many questions for Mr. Simpson. He explained that he had given Marty his business card the night of the play and had asked him to call him if he had any information to share. He went on to explain that he'd taken the copy of the jeweled mask the night of the play. "I brought it to a jeweler in town to ask if anyone had brought such a mask or perhaps the gems from the mask into his store with the intention of selling it."

"And I guess the reason you were at the costume store was to pick up your palace guard costume, right?" Barbie asked.

"Precisely!" Mr. Simpson replied. "It's my pleasure to meet you," he said formally.

Barbie eyed the man suspiciously, but then began to laugh. "The pleasure's all mine," she said, shaking his hand.

Mrs. Wellington wasted no time in inspecting the real mask and returning it to the display case along with the others. All the guests gathered in the collection room to see all the masks together again.

As the crowd "oohed" and "aahhhed" over the beautiful masks, there was one more surprise awaiting them. "Ladies and gentlemen, kings and queens," Mrs. Wellington declared, "please give a warm welcome to another surprise guest. Here to star in the next performance of *The Masked Stranger*, Ms. Angela Ames!"

Cheers filled Mrs. Wellington's home. "Thank you, Barbie," she said sincerely. "Thank you for bringing our stars back to us."

Barbie blushed modestly. Brian came to the rescue. "May I have this dance?" he asked.

"What about your two left feet?" Barbie asked, laughing.

Brian laughed, too. "All right, then, care to dance *at your own risk*?"

"I'd love to," Barbie replied, allowing her friend to pull her onto the ballroom floor.

Kira and Becky smiled as they watched their friend dance. "She's really amazing, isn't she?" Becky said. "She seems to be a mystery magnet!"

Kira giggled as she saw Barbie deftly step out of the way of her dance partner's feet. "I think she's more than just a mystery magnet," Kira said. "She's also a magnet for Brian's feet!"

The masquerade ball lasted until well after midnight. As the group of friends headed out together, Barbie looked up and saw that the sky was filled with twinkling lights. "Oh, look at all those beautiful stars!" she exclaimed.

Kira and Becky smiled at their friend. They knew in their hearts that Barbie would always be the brightest shining star of all.

Reporter's Notebook

Can YOU solve *The Mystery of the Jeweled Mask*? Read the notes below. Collect more notes of your own. Then, YOU solve it!

Story Assignment: Cover the opening of the new show, *The Masked Stranger*; write about the show and the jeweled mask worn by the star, Angela Ames.

● ●

Background Info:

● Mrs. Harris Wellington is the founder of the Wellington Foundation charity, owner of antique mask collection; the showpiece of the collection is the jeweled mask.

● The jeweled mask, valued at more than one million dollars, will go to London as part of the Jewels of the World exhibit after the run of the show is finished.

● A masquerade ball is to be held at Mrs. Wellington's house; all the money raised by the theater and charity ball will go to her charity foundation.

Mystery:

Who: Who stole the jeweled mask? Who locked Kira in the closet?

What: What connection does the man in the suit have with the stagehand Marty?

How: How did Diva Denton get a part in the show?

Where: Where is the mask now?

Why: Why does the man in the suit show up everywhere Barbie goes?

Facts and Clues:

- Angela Ames was called away by a note that turns out to be a hoax.
- Diva Denton — where did she come from?
- Man in the suit passes something to stagehand.
- Man in the suit disappears.
- Costume company connection
- Masks, real and fake

Suspects

- Diva Denton/Trixie Denton, understudy
- Man in suit, drives black sports car
- Marty, the stagehand

```
Additional Notes:

Clue #1 _____
_____
_____

Clue #2 _____
_____
_____

Clue #3 _____
_____
_____

Clue #4 _____
_____
_____

Clue #5 _____
_____
_____

Clue #6 _____
_____
_____
```

Now YOU Solve It!

_____
_____
_____
_____
_____
_____
_____
_____
_____
_____
_____
_____
_____
_____
_____
_____
_____
_____
_____
_____
_____
_____
_____
_____
_____

CONGRATULATIONS from BARBIE! You are an Official Star Reporter and Mystery Solver! Sharpen your mystery-solving wits and get ready to help Barbie solve her next big case.